The Accident

Library of Congress Cataloging in Publication Data
Carrick, Carol.   The accident.
Summary: After his dog is hit by a truck and killed, Christopher
must deal with his own feelings of depression and guilt.
[1. Death—Fiction. 2. Dogs—Fiction]   I. Carrick, Donald. II. Title.
PZ7.C2344Ac   [E]   76-3532   ISBN: 0-395-28774-X

The Accident

by CAROL CARRICK

pictures by DONALD CARRICK

Houghton Mifflin/Clarion Books/New York

It had rained all day at the summer cottage until dinnertime. After the dishes were washed Christopher's father said,

"The lake is smooth as glass. Let's go for a canoe paddle."

But Christopher's favorite television program was starting so he and his dog Bodger stayed home while his mother and father drove off.

When the program ended, Christopher and Bodger started down the dirt road to meet Christopher's parents. They would be driving back from the lake by now.

Bodger galloped ahead, the tags on his collar jingling. Now and then he stopped and looked back at Christopher as if to say, Hurry up! Sometimes he cut off into the brush, setting off a shower of droplets from the smaller trees.

Christopher wondered why his parents were taking so long. He and Bodger had reached the paved road and still there was no sign of their car.

Christopher walked in the soft dirt along the highway. Some of the people waved to him as they drove by. The faster cars and trucks made so much noise and wind when they passed that Christopher thought the blast might knock him over.

It was getting dark by the time he and Bodger neared the lake. How surprised his parents would be when they found him waiting at the boat landing. Maybe they would give him a canoe ride.

Then Christopher heard the pickup truck coming down the road.

Bodger was trotting along the other side of the road. Christopher called him to come over and stay next to him, but Bodger waited too long. He stopped a moment to sniff at something. Then he bounded into the road.

The truck's tires screeched as the driver swerved to avoid hitting the dog. Christopher's shoulders hunched and his eyes squeezed shut.

"BODGER!"

There was a thump, a high yelp from Bodger, and the truck came to a stop on the side of the road. Christopher couldn't believe it had really happened, but it had. He could see Bodger's legs twitch as if he were still running, and then the dog lay still.

Christopher started toward Bodger but he was afraid to touch him, afraid he might hurt him. The driver jumped out of the truck and ran to kneel beside the dog. He raised his hand as if to hold Christopher back.

Christopher already knew, but he asked anyway.

"Is he dead?"

The man shook his head sadly.

"I'm sorry, sonny."

The man was bringing a blanket from his truck just as Christopher's parents pulled up. Christopher ran toward them.

"Bodger's dead! That man hit him with his truck."

Christopher hoped that everything would turn out all right now. Somehow his Dad would take care of things.

"I didn't see him," the man explained as Christopher's father looked down at the dog and then covered him with the blanket. "He just suddenly ran in front of the truck."

His father silently nodded in understanding, but Christopher was disappointed. He was hoping his father would find that it was all a mistake, that Bodger was going to be O.K. At least he wanted his father to get mad at this man and tell him he would be punished for what he did. Instead, his father was agreeing with the man, feeling sorry for him. He didn't even care about Bodger.

The man squatted next to Christopher.

"I know just how you feel, sonny. I have two dogs at home. One of them has puppies. Would you like to come over in a few days and pick out a nice little puppy?"

"I don't want a puppy. I want Bodger," wailed Christopher. "And you killed him!"

"Christopher, Christopher," his mother soothed, as she led him to their car. "The man didn't mean to."

Suddenly the feeling that this was all just a dream ended. Christopher was angry. It wasn't fair. Why did that dumb man have to hit Bodger?

"I ought to run *him* over with a truck."

"Oh, honey, Bodger ran right in front of him. The man didn't have time to stop."

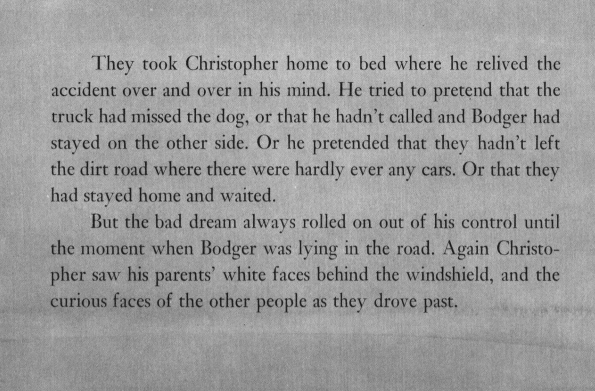

They took Christopher home to bed where he relived the accident over and over in his mind. He tried to pretend that the truck had missed the dog, or that he hadn't called and Bodger had stayed on the other side. Or he pretended that they hadn't left the dirt road where there were hardly ever any cars. Or that they had stayed home and waited.

But the bad dream always rolled on out of his control until the moment when Bodger was lying in the road. Again Christopher saw his parents' white faces behind the windshield, and the curious faces of the other people as they drove past.

Christopher woke late. For just a second he didn't remember the reason why a cold nose had not nudged him awake. But the recollection of last night came rushing into the summer morning and he knew that he would never see Bodger again.

When he entered the kitchen he stole a look at the corner where Bodger's bowls always sat, but they were gone. His father was still at the table although he had finished eating.

"Hi, Chrisso."

"Chrisso" had been Christopher's baby name for himself. His father hardly ever used it any more.

"I waited for you," his father said. "Do you want to come fishing with me?"

Christopher knew his father never went fishing this late in the morning.

"No thanks," he mumbled.

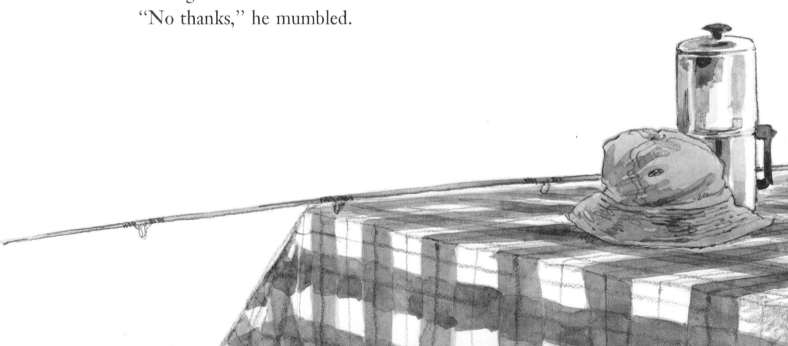

"How about some French toast?" his mother offered. "... with jelly on it."

"I don't want anything."

Christopher went out and sat on the steps. Bodger used to lie across the top step, ignoring the red squirrels that scolded him from the trees. Everybody always complained that he was in the way. Well, now they wouldn't have to complain.

His father came out and sat with him. Neither of them said anything for a while. Finally Christopher got up the courage to ask, "What did you do with Bodger?"

"I buried him near the brook."

"You buried him! Why didn't you tell me?"

"I didn't think you would want to be there, Christopher."

"Of course I did!" Christopher exploded angrily. "He was my dog. Why did you go and bury him without me? You didn't care about him. You don't care about me, either."

He didn't stay to hear his father's reply.

"Christopher! Wait a minute."

Christopher's face burned and the blood pounded in his ears as he stamped down the road. After a while he slowed down and the jumble of angry words he was muttering ran out. He turned back to the house, wondering what he was going to do now.

His father was still sitting on the steps. Christopher felt embarrassed. He was afraid to see his father's face.

"Christopher, why don't we take the canoe along the shore and find a nice stone to mark Bodger's grave."

During hundreds of years, their brook had tumbled and polished the rocks scattered along its course. At first Christopher didn't feel much enthusiasm. But as they paddled to the place where the brook emptied into the lake, he became excited about picking out the perfect stone for Bodger.

Sunlight danced off the ripples on the lake and glimmered
on the beached canoe and the two of them as they scrambled
over the rocks. Christopher called to his father from time to time
to examine a stone that seemed special.

It was difficult to decide. But then Christopher saw the stone
half buried in the bank. It had white lines running through it that
looked like the birch trees around the brook. They dug away
the earth and washed the stone before carefully lowering it into
the canoe.

When the stone was in place at the foot of Bodger's grave, Christopher didn't know what to say. But his father did.

"Remember how he used to come here on a hot day for a drink, and wade in that icy water? And how he'd see the little trout and try to pounce on one? Then he would stop to look around and wonder why all the fish had disappeared."

Christopher giggled. The giggle turned into a sob. He began to cry, and then cry hard. It felt good this time.

"Oh, Dad!"

His father put an arm around Christopher's shoulders. Christopher turned and let the strong arms enfold him. He didn't feel angry with his father any more, and that felt good, too.